The
Centurion
Captive

By. M. Francis Lamont

Dedicated

with love
to the divine memory of
Devika
Mother of Vikkas
The wonderful man on the cover.

Thank you Vikkas for the gift of the cover image. You bring beauty to the world and peace to those around you.

Hedda, my friend. I love that this is the first cover you ever designed for me and is, amusingly, the last piece of yours that I am privileged to publish. Your talent is undeniable.

To my friends who support my dream and the readers who encourage me every day:

Thank you.

Please don't forget to post your reviews anywhere and everywhere. They are more important than you know.

Ch 1

It had all gone so wrong. Julius had sat for hours the night before, after they had thrown him in the cell made of fire hardened wood, trying to discern where his reconnaissance mission plan had gone wrong.

Where was the flaw?

The area had been scouted by Septus and the man had never made a mistake in choosing a lookout location before. The hills had been perfectly sculpted, as though the gods themselves had chosen them and designed the bushes and the land for just such a purpose. Even his commanding officer had agreed, readily, that he had planned everything to perfection. The only way that they could have been discovered was if the gods hated him or they had been betrayed.

"Wake. Roman scum!" The sound of metal against the chains above his head and the coarse voice with the thick accent was just enough to wake him from the light sleep he was trying to convince himself he was dreaming in. He had tried to force himself to sleep near dawn, which was only hours ago by the looks of the sky

"I 'woke'. Damned savage." He grumbled under his breath. Their lack of knowledge of his language made it likely that the guard had not understood him. The Gauls were as ignorant as they were stubborn, the reasons that Rome thought they could conquer them and the reason that they could not, perfectly outlined in a single thought.

"You should be careful." Said a feminine voice behind the guard. "Callo will not like what you call him when he understands your tongue better." He turned his head to find the source of the voice as he replied. "I do not think I will care if he does. He is not likely to ever understand it, unless you tell him what it means as you seem to have a better grasp it yourself."

He finally managed to turn over. The chains were not easy to maneuver with, especially bound at the wrists, but what was standing before his bars made him forget everything he had been thinking.

Beneath the shawl covering her head were curling wisps of hair the color of golden fire framing a pale delicate face with a pointed chin. Full berry colored lips frowned at him beneath a sprinkling of freckles that accented eyes as green as emeralds. She was glaring at him but instead of feeling angry Julius felt a need to make her smile.

"Do you? Understand my tongue?" He asked with a grin as he briefly thought about what he would do with his tongue if she were his woman or at least in his bed. It had been weeks since they had been anywhere that had women who were not the whores that had been used by every man that could get near them. He was not a man that shared with others. Anything, anyone, that he treasured was his alone. "Do you want to learn more of it?"

She scoffed with the slightest shake of her head, letting a few more curls fall free of the cloth in spirals so tight he wanted to tug one straight to see it bounce back to its form.

"There is nothing else of your language that I need to know. Romans are cruel and violent. You are heartless people. Death is what you deserve." She said with the accent that did not sound harsh or foolish from her lips.

What was wrong with him? He was lusting after the enemy. It had to be the lack of a decent woman in weeks. It could not be the fact that he had never seen a woman with eyes and hair like this. The fact that he wanted to devour her lips and make her close those sparkling emeralds as she gasped in passionate exclamation was simply due to the fact that she was different than the whores that had been trailing the legion for months.

"There are many things that you could learn about my language. Not all of us are cruel even if we are slightly violent." He sat up a little more, looking up at her from his seat on the ground. "You think I deserve death? For what crime do I deserve it? I am just a man who followed orders to find information. I have done you no harm in this life and I do not desire to."

She laughed and him, crouching low to meet his eyes. "You are the enemy. The enemy of my people. You are here to kill the men and make the women, to make me, a slave to your will. For that you deserve death, as much as my people would deserve death if they did the same to your country. Would you not wish the same for Callo if he were in your place and you in his?"

He could not deny that was the reality of their allegiances but how many men brought home foreign wives from war? What would have to happen for her to leave with him when he eventually returned to Rome, leaving her people unconquered? The reality of that thought suddenly made him cough. He had never given such a position thought let alone considered someone to hold that title in his life. Why did this tiny woman, a Gaul of all people, staring down at him through the bars of his cell where he was captive to her tribe, put thoughts of marriage in his mind.

"I wish no man a death he has not earned." That was a simple truth that he had been taught as a young boy by the soldier that was his hero.

"Then I hope you have not earned it, Roman." She said, standing to look down on him once again. "I shall ask that you be spared the fate of the others. They were not as you are. One of them stole the knife from a guard and put it in his back. They fought, two Romans against us, they did not win. You are all that is left to answer the questions of the chief."

She did not give him the chance to answer but turned, leaving him to absorb that information that he was alone in the enemy territory. His friends were dead, two of them at least. Maybe one had gotten away? She hadn't mentioned the fourth Roman and he knew that they had found all four hiding spots. They would not risk storming the camp just to save him, but there was still a chance that they might want to use the intelligence gathered if someone made it back. If anyone had it would have been Cato. People assumed that it was because he was an animal in the battlefield, but it was because he was able to move like the animals, unseen and quick through day or night.

It had to be Cato that survived, which meant Septus and Linus, two of his closest friends in this world, were gone. Dead at the hands of the men around him. Her men, her family and those that she called friend. A blanket of hatred settled over him for all those around him. From the guards at the gates who looked back at him with a smugness that he now understood to the children returning with firewood in their arms and the women near the well whispering. Was it about him? He was the sole surviving Roman spy they had captured. They had killed the others, likely while they were trapped within the cells, unable to run. They had no chance but a swift death that no one would ever know of because they had been betrayed by man or the gods.

Julius hung his head in a moment of mourning for those that were lost. Vengeance would come and he prayed that the gods let his hands be their instrument to rain it down upon the heads of the guilty. Pressing his palms to his eyes, Julius released a ragged breath. He would not give them the satisfaction of tears or the show of his emotions.

How could they be gone? Until moments ago, he had been listening for the voices of his comrades. He had been waiting to hear them tease him for the foolish sound of his voice. They would have known what he was saying and would never have let him hear the end of it. Now he would never hear them again and that knowledge alone almost broke him. For the first time in his life Julius was alone. He had never been alone in his life, growing up with brothers and a sister with a large family of her own children had not left much time to be alone.

"Barbarian bastards." He growled, fighting to stifle his emotions. He would not break for them.

Rubbing a hand down his face Julius raised his eyes to meet those of his mysterious fire haired woman. The emerald gaze was sad, sympathetic, but it was still the enemy's face. Though it was the most beautiful he could remember this was not Rome and there was no one coming to save him this time.

"You will pay for their deaths...someday." He muttered under his breath

He sighed, looking around him at the cell. The bars were fire-hardened spikes of wood that went high above his head, with a thatched roof pierced in a few places that would likely let rain pour down on him. If he was alive when it rained again.

The day passed without any other words or visitors to his cell. He managed to stretch his arms and legs but standing upright was impossible due to the chain attached to the collar around his neck. Had they added the collar after the death of his friends, or had it been there all along? It did not take a genius to know that it was there to stop him from getting to his feet and walking around the cell. Did that mean they thought he was more dangerous than the others or that they, his friends, had they died barely able to move? Because they defied their captors?

"I will show you the meaning of defiance." He muttered to himself with sudden inspiration. He would win the trust of one of his captors so that they would let him stand, perhaps walking among them until they forgot that he was a Roman enemy. That was when he would set fire to the village, escaping in the chaos with their greatest treasure.

Julius sat as still as possible for the rest of the day, mostly feigning sleep to watch those around him to see if he could discover what the greatest treasure of this tribe was. They did not seem to have a temple within the confines of the village, that would have been an obvious choice to hide their treasures. He wondered perhaps if there was a priestess or priest? Their chief would be a great warrior and not easy to take with him. They would trust that their leader could free himself or he would not be a worthy chief. No, he sighed in frustration and hunger, he needed something irreplaceable; rare and valuable.

"Roman scum." Callo's rough voice brought him back to the moment. "Eat. Then I take you. You will see our chief. Answer for your crimes to him."

Wordlessly Julius choked back the dry food and the water then waited for the collar to be unlocked so that he could be walked, under guard, to see the Chief of these savages. Perhaps this would give him the sight of the treasure that he needed.

"Roman ate. Shall we go then?" He replied, staying calm while they unfastened the chain, but not the collar holding him in place and lifted him to his feet. Thankfully, they allowed him to stretch completely once he was free of the cell. They used the opportunity to search him for hidden weapons again.

Once they started to walk it did not take long to reach the largest hut in the village. Long, taller than the other structures, it was conveniently located directly behind his cell. That was why he had not been able to see the structure of obvious significance.

They paused outside the wide door made of curtains that looked like thick wool, with a layer of leather to keep out the cold. This would be the most important meeting of his life, at least for the present.

"Chief will see Roman scum. No words from you. Wait for his words first." Were the rough instructions growled in his ear before they walked through the door.

"So, this is the sole remaining Roman prisoner to answer for the actions against my people." A deep voice boomed from the far end of the hall. "This is the man that lives simply because I am told he is valuable. A man with answers I was told."

Julius started to look up as the voice continued but his head was shoved back down. "Give answers, Roman. Why should you live? What information do you have that I might value enough to balance scales against your life?"

"I do not know who told you such lies, but I have no words or answers to give to you." He was allowed to look up at last and what he saw took his breath away. It was not the lavish surroundings, or the feast he appeared to be interrupting, it was the occupant in seat at the left hand of the chief.

Head bared with those fiery curls cascading down over her shoulders, glowing in the torchlight, staring at him, sat the woman from that morning. The one that stirred his lust sat at the hand of his captor.

"You, Roman, breaker of promises, dare to name her a liar? You say this of my daughter?"

Ch 2

Julius was stunned to silence for a moment. The woman was the daughter of his captor? The murderer of his companions? She must want him dead as much as the rest of the villagers, so then why did she tell his father that he had value? That he had information he could and would trade for his life? Why did she lie and how did she dare to meet his eye across a room filled with her people and with rage of her father vibrating through the space?

"I do not name her so, sir." Julius said, trying to remain calm in the face of the extreme hostility. "There is just the difference in tongue that brings me to believe that the girl misunderstood my words. How much could she have understood of what a man of war says?"

He had thought to find some common ground with the men in the room, reminding them that war and its language was not a thing for the soft hearted, emotional mind of a woman. He did not expect the immediate, thundering reaction from all sides. He did not understand the words but it was clear that they were insulted by his words excluding the females in the room from knowledge and participation in matters of war.

How could he have forgotten that these Gaulish tribes involved their women in aspects of their lives in ways that Romans never considered. They went to war beside their men. He should have known that the girl was likely spying on him to get information for the chief, but it did not make sense that she told them that he was valuable. He was no one of any worth to these people or even his own.

Julius was under no illusion that he was a soldier of any greatness. Despite his drive and desire, he was not destined for command. At the end of this campaign, if he survived which was not likely now, he would be lucky to serve as a private guard to some lesser senator. He did not relish the disdain he would receive from his family at such a low posting, but now it did not seem that he would have to worry about that until they joined him in the afterlife these barbarians would shortly dispatch him to.

"My daughter knows more of the Roman tongue that you suppose, Centurion." The Chief laughed. "You will tell me the secrets of the legion. I want to know their position and what they want. I want to know why they have not sent men to bargain for your life and for the bodies of their dead."

The big man leaned forward on his ornately carved wooden chair and beckoned for Julius' guards to bring him closer. When he was near enough to see the sweat beading on the broad forehead of his captor and the ragged, nervous breath of the young woman who could barely meet his eyes, he decided then to take fate into his own hands.

"I have no wish to return to the legion and this is known to them. I cannot fight with the fools who think that they will concern the barbarian hordes of Gaulia. I will tell you what I know, if only you do not send me back to them, to that place. I would stay here in your village until you see fit to release me and then I will wander the wild until the gods direct me. They have told me to turn from Rome and thus they have delivered me to you."

The room fell to a stunned silence, so much so that Julius could have sworn he heard his red-haired beauty whisper.

"Thank the gods."

When he glanced up her brilliant green eyes flicked immediately down to the ground and away from his inquisitive stare. She was a mystery to him and, if he survived the night, he would find the truth from her. Unravelling her just as she did to his senses that morning in the cage.

"Your gods brought you to us? To my village? They must mean for you to help us to wipe the Roman scum from my countryside. Send them back to Rome and Germania where they might win against those savages." The chief looked around the room while his warriors laughed, including those holding on the Julius with a slightly looser grip now.

"Or is this a trick of Rome? Like the horse of the Trojans, are you here to destroy my home by fooling us into trusting you?"

"No. Never. I have no wish to return to Rome. Their world, their laws, are no longer my own." He could almost hear the curses of his parents at his words, but it was the only chance he had to live to see them again. "I will not go back. How can I prove that to you?"

He was shocked by the silence in the room that followed his declaration but there was a thoughtful look on the face of the chief that gave him a sliver of hope that they might take him seriously and give him the chance that he needed to plan his escape. If he was going to survive this place, this test, he was going to have to be charming and listen to everything around him. He could return to the legion with the information that could annihilate these people and secure him the promotion he desired.

"You want to prove yourself to us? To these people that you would call your own? I will think upon it, then we will all decide." The group roared their approval which only got louder when the chief added "While we make our choice you will wait back where Roman scum belong."

Before he could say anything else, protesting or agreeing, Julius found himself being dragged from the warm room. Instead of the light and the smell of food that left his senses reeling, he was back in the cold dark of the night then he tossed roughly back into the cage of polished wooden bars and packed dirt floor. They did not refasten the shackles or attach the chain to his neck which gave him hope for the decision that they would make. He would either be granted life or sent to his death before the sun rose and even the gods could not have told him which it would be now. His fate was in their hands, and perhaps the hands of the red-haired siren.

Settling his back against the bars he wondered again at her words. He had thought that, perhaps, there had been a connection between them and the lie she had told to the chief, her own father, for him seemed to agree with that suggestion.

"I do not know if I should thank or curse you, woman of fire." He muttered to himself, looking up through the bars to gaze at the stars above him. They were so different than the ones at home, yet the months in the area made them at least familiar. The clouds danced across the surface of the moon before clearing the sky so that every star sparked, lighting the night so that it was almost bright enough to see across the square to where his fate was being decided. It was also dark enough to hide his actions if he moved slow enough. Dipping the tips of his fingers into the top of his grieves Julius pulled the spear tip he kept hidden there whenever he was away from home. It had been given to him by his hero to keep him safe from suffering the same fate he had suffered until his death. Slavery after being taken prisoner of war.

The man had been no common slave or a gladiator, but an officer of the legion. A legend. An unrivaled warrior for the Republic, Titus Claudius was everything, had everything, that Julius wanted for his own career and life. The highlight of his youth had been when, after the parade celebrating the defeat of another enemy of Rome, the hero had opened the gates of his estate and welcomed some of the young men to meet him and his squad of heroes. That meeting had changed the way the young man viewed service in the legion and had driven him to learn how to fight in the manner of his hero. He credited the Centurion for inspiring him to fight and find his purpose in the legion.

Looking at the weapon Julius remembered the moment it had been placed in his hands and the promise that had been given over the exchange.

Ch 3

"There he is. There he is" Ten-year-old Julius screamed from atop his father's shoulders. The soldier seemed to have heard him for he thrust the spear in his hand high in the air bringing a roar from the crowd. The young boy cheered so loudly that even the adults in the front row of the parade turned to look at him.

"Do truly you think he heard me father?" Julius said while he was lifted from his shoulders to be set on the edge of the street.

"Well I would look at the street and find that out for yourself." His father said, gesturing to the procession where Titus Claudius was pointing the shining weapon towards the young boy.

"For the Republic!" Titus bellowed. The crowd in the street and those up in the windows joined in the sound and Julius mirrored the gesture back to his idol.

It was a moment later that his father whispered for Julius to look away from Titus towards two men in uniform that were selecting young men from the crowd to join the end of the parade. A runner from the front of the column joined the soldiers delivered a quick message then ran back the way that he had come. Both men were grinning as they scanned the crowd, obviously looking for someone specific. Suddenly they were pointing at him and gesturing Julius forward from the crowd and out onto the road.

"Father? Am I in trouble? Should I not have been so loud? Did I bring offence?" His voice was filled with worry while his father guided him through the crowd.

"No boy but it seems to me that you have caught the attention of an important person." His father smiled warmly down at him. "Let us see what his interest has in store for you? Shall we?" His voice sounded calm, but his eyes were just as nervous as Julius felt.

In the street, with the other youngsters, the centurion guard waited for them. A few people had lingered to see what would happen to the noisy young boy that had been so enthusiastic. The legionnaires were not known to enjoy children at the best of times and the citizens wanted to bear witness to any roughness the young innocent was treated with.

Julius, clinging to his father's hand, was still nervous that he was about to be punished for being a distraction to the great, distinguished warrior during the celebration.

"Father? Don't let them hurt me." He said softly, wishing he could hide or turn and run home but that would leave his father to answer for the offences of his son.

"I doubt that they have the thought to harm you child." His father said, sharing a nod with the soldier. "I want you to pay attention and be careful not to offend."

"Yes father." Julius nodded, trying his best to appear calm and not as nervous as he felt. He quickly fell in step with the other boys as they followed the soldiers leading them towards his hero.

"You stand an admirer of Titus, young man?" An old soldier asked once the gates of the great estate closed behind the last of the children and the heroes began to mingle with the younger generation. "My son Markus was your age when he discovered his first hero among the ranks. It is a grand moment in a young man's life when he finds his path."

"Yes, sir." Julius said. His shyness forgotten as he delved into his favorite subject. "When I am old enough to join the legion, I want to be just like him I think the gods themselves pause in the heavens to watch when the great Titus Claudius goes into battle. There is no other man in the whole Republic that fights as he can."

He jumped into a fighting stance and pretended to wield a sword and began to display his attempt at the skills of a Centurion in battle. "When he makes the death blow all the heavens hear the cry and I cannot help but imagine the sound."

Julius stopped suddenly, as the men around him chuckled "Is that why you wish to break words? Was I too loud? Did I bring offence to you or Centurion Claudius with my distraction?"

"Not at all young man. Julius is your given name is it not?" The senior soldier asked, smiling while he put a hand on his shoulder. "I have an idea. Would the fan of the hero like to meet the man himself?"

While Julius gaped in surprise. "May I really? Speak with him? Shake his hand?" Julius looked back and forth between the man he was speaking to and the one that he desired to meet. "I may meet Titus Claudius himself?"

"Yes, dear boy. He awaits you now." Tertius said, gesturing for the boy to follow him across the yard.

The grass was crisp and fresh beneath his feet and the voices of the other boys talking amongst themselves as well as the soldiers toasting each other in victory was loud and echoing through the walled space. Julius was too excited to be bothered by the sound, his focus was on his hero alone. "Do you think he will show me how to fight? Even just a few strikes?" He asked, hoping that he did not push his luck too far with such a question.

"I am sure that Titus would enjoy teaching you a thing or two." The silver-haired soldier said, tapping the man in question upon the shoulder. "Titus, before you find yourself too familiar with the wine there is someone hoping to break words with you."

With his spear in one hand and a glass of wine in the other Titus turned to meets Julius' eyes with a mischievous smile. "Well now, who is this young man? Is this the one who yells so loudly for the glory of Rome and our great victory?"

"He stands the very one Titus. I think that the parents of these young recruits will be here soon, and I should be the one to meet them at the gates. I shall return after they seen to." He spoke over Julius' head to his fellow soldier. "They are annoying at best, but the sooner they allow us to begin training these boys the better soldiers they will be when we need them to be."

He walked off, leaving young Julius face to face with his hero. Stepping towards him Julius found himself suddenly feeling shy and very much the child that he was. "Is it still sharp? Your spear?" he asked, pointing towards the weapon.

"It is young man, but it is heavier than it is sharp." The Centurion held out the weapon for him to take into his own hands. "Would you like to hold it?

Julius held his hand out to take the weapon into his hand, surprise at the weight on his face. "This is the same one that you used in the recent battle? Has it killed many men? For more years than I have been alive, this spear has been taking lives. You have been using this very one to kill in the battlefield."

"Yes, young warrior," Titus said with a smile. "That is the very one I used in my latest victory. It is one of three that I use."

Julius watched as Titus struck a pose to strike an invisible opponent. "Stand as I stand boy. I will position the spear for you. Just as I am, then you will know what it is like to stand, ready to take a life."

Ready in moments Julius was worried that he was going to drop the spear which was heavier than he thought it would be. His hands were shaking when Titus stood behind him, close enough that he could smell the hint of wine on his breath. When Titus reached over his shoulders to grasp the weapon Julius was not sure that he would be able to concentrate in such close proximity to his hero. He did not know if he had the strength to move as the soldier did.

"Steady now. You are strong enough if you pull from deep within. You have strength you do not realize. Use it and use it well." Titus said quietly, molding Julius' position into the needed stance and helping him support the weapon.

"You're right. I can feel the strength in that position more. You have used this many times Titus?"

The gladiator laughed and nodded before easing the him into another position. They continued this, posing in position, and practicing the death strike needed for each of them. Each new one brought laughter and the tale of how it was used once in the battlefield. Julius knew that no matter what other things happened to him in his life he was never going to forget this day and these lessons.

Julius had just taken the spear back in his hand, spinning it with a new confidence, when his father, the older soldier and another officer of the legion all joined them with broad smiles.

"Father! Look what Titus taught me." He leaped into an attack stance. "He said that I have a deep strength." He missed the nod between his father and his hero when he proudly displayed another pose for the members of the legion who showered him with praise for his quick learning of the new skills.

"It is time that we depart Julius." His father said, putting a hand to his shoulder. "Let us leave these men of war to the victory celebrations that Titus and the others deserve. You have lessons tomorrow with your tutor and will need a good night's sleep after this excitement."

"Yes father." He said, shoulders slumping just a little. "Thank you, Centurion, for the lessons. I will not forget what you have taught me today." He bowed his head in respect before handing back the spear he held carefully in his still eager hands.

"You should keep that, young Julius." Titus said with a sudden smile and shake of his head "Your hand is suited to it and it will help a young mind remember lessons taught longer than the memory of words alone."

"Thank you, oh, thank you." Julius said, surprise on his face. He rushed to the soldier and threw his arms around him "I will never forget, this or you. Never."

Ch 4

Julius woke to the vibration of the bars being kicked near his head and a deep voice calling. "Roman wake. Food, then work." He opened his eyes to see the same guard as the night before glaring down at him. "Wake, eat, work." He said again, clearly struggling with the language. "Work or die. You choose." He said, placing a bowl of hot mash, a small loaf of bread and a jug of clear cold water on the ground.

"I wake, I wake." Julius grumbled as he sat up. "Of all in this place you are the first that I would raise arms against if I was given a single moment with a weapon in hand."

"Roman will eat and then work. I take you. Planting seed, your work will feed us in winter." Callo said with a devious smile.

Julius ate as quickly as he could and stepped to the side of the cell furthest from where he slept to relieve himself while his guard unlocked the simple door that locked him within the cell.

"I would blight the seed if I knew how. Instead I will petition the gods to stunt their growth when the harvest comes." He said to himself while he followed the guard to the field where he would either work or die.

Julius took in every part of the scene around him, trying to memorize not only the faces but the trees as well, and the paths. The field was surrounded by trees and he was surprised to see that it was being tilled by his own horse. He had thought the animal would have either been killed or sent to the chief for his use alone.

"Our chief has decided that since you come from a people who take their prisoners to be slaves that you will learn what it is that they feel when you take their freedom. With the loss of your own you might grow to be a better man before you meet your gods." The man who was obviously in charge said, with his arms crossed over his chest.

With a deep frown on his face Julius began the work, at least now he knew that they meant to kill him at some point.

"They can try to strip me of my identity, but my will can outlast their vigilance. Then we will ride for Rome and freedom." He said with a smile, tickling the charger behind his ear as he knew the big horse liked.

"Horses are the best judges of a man, after dogs of course." Said a soft voice from the other side of the animal. "Maybe you are not the cruel monsters that my father declares all Romans to be."

The voice belonged to the chieftain's daughter who must have come out of the trees to stroke the horse opposite him. As much as he was drawn to her Julius wanted to hate her. If he failed at that he had to, at least, keep her far enough away that he could pretend to hate her completely.

"You are a fool, woman. I am every inch the monster he thinks I am. Every breath, every thought is set upon the death of all who stand between me and freedom." He growled in return, determined to keep his attraction to her hidden when she looked into his eyes.

"You plot my death, Roman?" She asked, looking up at him, fearless but curious.

Perhaps the proximity of the guards made her bold or perhaps she simply did not fear him. He could not be sure, but he admired her bravery.

"You, and the boy with the water, are the only ones I would spare if you stood between me and freedom to return home." He said roughly, stepping away from her intoxicating presence to begin his work as she sat to watch him. He felt as if he were in the training yard of his youth but instead of swords, he held the reins of a plow. With each step he deepened his thoughts of escape, forcing those of the flame-haired girl aside except when the dream included taking her with him. As a hostage for his safety or as a willing companion he did not dare question.

Days turned to weeks and little changed except that she came to visit Julius daily and he had finally learned her name; Tanaquil. It was as foreign to him as her country and customs, but once he learned how to say it, he found that he enjoyed the sound of it. Just as surprising he found that he was starting to enjoy the country around him. He could almost say that he was falling in love and not just with the beauty of his captive nation. Tanaquil was kind-hearted and yet every man he saw treated her with the respect he was used to seeing shown to the Senators or Generals in his country. He had never known anyone like her, man, or woman. She could speak of plants and their uses just as easily as she discussed the philosophy of war. More than once he smiled at the thought of taking her to a council of the elders at home and watching every man stare in amazement and then growing respect for his woman.

He found himself thinking of her as his more and more often. In every dream that he had of freedom she was at his side, his Queen, as intelligent as she was ravishingly beautiful. He would proudly walk the streets of his capital with her beside him. He would even stay and join her people if he thought they would accept him. As it was, he was still sure that they meant to kill him if there was no chance for a ransom.

It was almost mid-day. The sun was as high as it got this far north of the Roman territories and he knew that Tanaquil would arrive at the field soon with the mid-day meal. It was the second-best part of his day. The only part that was better was when she came to his cell to bring his evening food and water for the night. They no longer kept him under constant guard while locked behind the wooden bars. Callo barely even paused by him anymore and no longer threw stick and rocks to wake him as he had the first week of his captivity. If he did not know better, he would have guessed that the stubborn savage had begun to like him.

"Roman, stop. Eat now." His watchman called, the same stubborn pig from the first day.

"My name is Lucius, you stunned ass." He grumbled under his breath.

Every day it was the same. He knew that the man refused to call him by his name as a way of dehumanizing him. Many Romans did the same thing to their slaves, giving them 'proper' names to keep them in constant reminder of their lowered station.

"Your name is Roman, until it is dead Roman. It will matter no more after that." Was the reply he received, along with a hard smack to the back of his head as though he were a child to be chastised.

"Hey! Do not think to do that again or I will not be the only dead man." He turned to face his tormentor, annoyed and ready to finally put an end to the daily mockery. He had not understood what Titus had told him about the biggest burden that faced any solider once captured. It was not the threat of death or violent outbursts from their captors, but something deeper.

"No, my boy." He had said in his soft, calming voice on one of the many visits he had made to the barracks and sometimes his private villa over the years as he waited to be old enough to enlist. "No. The worst scene that can happen to you as a prisoner is that they win. That they take your humanity, you soul, along with your freedom. Only of one of those can be captured in a battle Julius. If a man loses who he is, then the journey to his recovery will never be easy and for some it will be impossible. Some men remain prisoners long after they are released by their captors."

These were the words ringing in his ears when he struck the taunting Gaul across his smug jaw. The big man hit the ground as though it had been a club and not a fist that struck him. Even as the other guards rushed to the fallen man's aid Julius laughed to himself. He did not move to attack the fallen man. He had more honor that that. He was certain that his point had been proven; he was still a man to be reckoned with, no matter his station.

A blow to the back of his knees too him to the ground with a grunt but he kept his head high and his fist unclenched. He would not give them further cause for violence, but would answer truthfully, if asked, that any man among them would have done the same. Once could only be pushed so far before it was time to react or be broken forever. He closed his eyes as several more blows rained down. Just when he thought he could take no more he heard a voice calling for them to halt.

She was there?

Tanaquil had saved him from her own people? He wondered, as he teetered on the edge of consciousness, if they would listen.

"If you beat him you had best be willing to do the work in his stead."

He could hear her voice, confident and commanding to the men around him. She was incredible. The men all stepped away and he could feel her approach and though he expected her to speak to him he was surprised when he felt soft, slender fingers threading through his hair.

Forcing his eyes open Julius looked up at her. "Gratitude." He said in a quiet voice. "I returned the blow that he gave for no reason besides my own name aloud. It was more than any man should be made to stand, to de deprived of his own name. I beg for understanding, since I cannot pray for forgiveness with the true hope of it's being granted.

There was some exchange of words between Tanaquil and the men that he could not understand but it seemed to him that she was pleading his case. He did not dare to stand, even when the others stepped away to return to their food. It was not until he heard her sigh that he relaxed and opened his eyes to look at her.

"I know that it was foolish, but it could not be helped. I will not let him take my humanity. I would rather die." Julius said, sitting up.

"My Roman, I fear if you act so rashly again that you may see that wish granted. You play a dangerous game when you do these things."

He shook his head, surprised to notice that his once short jet-black hair now brushed his shoulders. Would the legions, his brothers in arms, even recognize him now? Would he be a stranger among his own people?

"I play no games Tanaquil. Even in my lands, my home, I never treated any slave as though they were not human. I would never treat a prisoner like this. There are nights I wish that I did not wake, that my gods would come for me in the night. Ending this captivity, one way or another, is almost the only thought that I have. The other is my gratitude for the only thing that makes some moments bearable."

He was ranting, perhaps speaking too fast for her to understand everything he said but the floodgate of his frustration was open now and it would not be closed until all was said aloud.

"I swear that you are the only light in the darkness that my life has become. I am supposed to die a warrior's death, not a slave denied any defence but my bare fists. I was ready to fight to my death until you stopped them."

He realized that in his frustration he had risen to his feet and was now so close that he was looming over her. A quick glance told him that the guards were watching him again. They were waiting to see if she thought him to be a threat, but the woman simply stared at him as though he had stars hung in his eyes instead of a hatred for his situation.

"I bring joy to your day? I thought you were annoyed by my questions about you and your home."

"You are the only one here who treats me like a man, Tanaquil. Why is that?" His tone had softened, and he wanted to smile at her reaction to the change in his demeanor. "Why do you bring my food when that is a task far below a Chieftain's daughter? To the fields and to my cell at night? There is never anyone but you. Can you tell me why?"

Every fiber in him wanted to reach out and stroke a strand of that fiery red gold hair from her face, but he did not dare move with eyes of the guards watching him with deadly intensity. Her cheeks flushed pink at his questions, and she looked like she was going to run.

"I..." Her answer was cut off by the arrival of a new Gaul stepping clear of the trees and walking straight up to Julius and Tanaquil.

"You are late Princess. We had agreed to meet for the midday meal and instead I find you lowering yourself by feeding the Roman cur. Has he brought you offence that I should see him brought down?"

Julius met his eyes, silently daring him try. He recognized that the man was as much a warrior as he was himself. If they both held a sword might even be able to offer a proper contest to the centurion's skills. The challenge charged the air between them, the unspoken claim of either man threatening to anoint the field with the blood of one warrior or another.

"No Quellus. All is dealt with here. I offer apologies. I had thought that meal was planned for tomorrow." Was her stilted reply.

The soft tone of moments before was gone, replaced with a coldness he had not yet heard from her. Returning her eyes to Julius he thought he saw regret shining at him when she continued.

"We can go eat now. There is nothing I have left to say to him."

Julius watched the pair leave together and sat back down to eat the food she had left for him.

The rest of the day was silent for him, even his guards were wisely silent, speaking only when it was time to stop for the day.

Ch 5

Trudging back to his cell Julius felt the inner fire of his earlier victory fading with the light of the sun. Of course, a woman with her prestige would be spoken for by the warrior of the tribe. He had been foolish to think the blush on her cheek was anything other than embarrassment at the absurdity of his words. It did not make the words or emotions any less true, but he should never have let himself believe it would matter, that he would matter to her.

"If the gods take me tonight, I will be laughed away from the gates of Elysium for such folly. To think I had convinced myself that I held meaning to her. That she saw a man and not a slave." He growled to himself in frustration.

"I see much more than a man, Julius. I see the soul of a Centurion who, even as a captive, is greater than that of any warrior I have ever met."

He looked up to meet the soft emerald gaze, surprise flooding him when he saw that it was not a dream.

"You hold meaning and I am the greater fool for it. It is madness to deny my father's blessed choice for a love that can never be fulfilled." Tanaquil said, stepping closer to the bars.

He was wrong, he had to be dreaming to hear such words from her lips. The brightness of the moon set her pale skin aglow with the light of Olympus.

"You would choose me if I stood a free man before you Tanaquil?" Julius asked, his voice a husky whisper through the night. He hoped to never wake if this were a dream and if it were a ploy to lead him to his death then he would die a happy man if he got to taste her lips even once.

"I choose you even now. We may never be together, but I choose you Julius."

He stood, towering over her petite frame once again and yet there was no fear, no distress, in her expression. It was clear that she meant what she had said, and his heart surged with joy.

There were only inches between them, and the bars did not seem to exist.

"Our fates are sealed, and the gods will guide us together in their time." He said, reaching out to do what he had wanted to do since he first lay eyes upon her.

Julius ran the tips of his fingers through her hair and across her cheek. She felt as smooth as marble but as soft as the petals of a rose. When he lowered his lips towards her, daring to hope that she might allow the chaste kiss that the cell would allow. She rose to meet him with an eagerness that surprised and delighted him to his core.

She tasted like the sweet red berries that grew in the woods beside the field he worked, but it was her soft moan that made him hungry for more. A sweep of his tongue parted her eager lips and deepened the kiss. His broad hands, accustomed to a tight grip on the sword he was now denied, were gentle as he spanned her waist and drew her closer. His own body was pressed against the wooden rods as near as he could be. He drank her in, savoring the taste of her kiss with every starved sweep of his tongue. It was only when she winced that he realized he had, in his eagerness, pulled her too hard against the bars.

"Apologies." He whispered. His voice rough with the desire to hold her with no barrier between them. "I did not mean to cause you pain, but you are water to a man parched with thirst. Tanaquil, I want to take you back with me to my home, to Rome. Would you run away with me?"

He watched her face as the suggestion, the request, sank in. Her eyes widened and a flush rose up her neck. It blossomed across her face so beautifully that Julius wanted to make it happen again and again. He wanted to see her in the morning light, laying beside him with that same glow lighting her face. To have her come home with him to the Republic would not be easy for either of them. She would be an outsider and he would have to work hard to help her find a place among the wives of the other soldiers. This was not the first time that he considered it a blessing from the gods that he was not a member of the elite of the city.

"You want me to leave with you? You do not even know me Julius. How can you be certain of such a thing?" She asked in a whisper so soft he could barely hear it.

"How can I be certain of anything? The same way that we are both certain that the sun will rise in the East tomorrow and set in the West. That is simply what will happen, what should happen. The only thing stopping it is your words." He clasped her hands in his, scratching the backs of his when he reached through the bars. "I want to be with you as I have never wanted anything in all my life. All you have to do is say that you want me, and I will find a way to break free of this captivity. I will happily risk my life for the chance to live the rest of it with you."

He stared down into her eyes and felt a surge of hope as a smile teased at the edge of her lips. She could honestly say yes. Give him the drive he needed to escape this place and take Tanaquil home to start a new life together. Every night together would be the realization of a dream and when her wild temper flared he would have the chance to sooth her and make her smile again. It would be better than even the dreams of his childhood to have her at his side.

She just had to say yes.

"There is nothing that I want more than to leave here with you and leave all this life behind. I do not know how it is that we shall accomplish this, but it is my desire as well." Tanaquil said with a soft smile that touched his heart.

"We will find a way. Soon we will be free of this place and far from it." Julius said, slipping the tip of his finger down her cheek. "We will be happy together."

"I believe that we can be, if we can get away from this place and my father." Tanaquil said with a flash of worry in her eyes that he wanted to eliminate entirely.

"It is not without complications. We will have to plan a route and I will have to escape this cage without drawing the attention of those who stand guard at night. Once we are a day, perhaps two, away from here then we will be safe. It is unlikely that they will follow us that far."

"How far is Rome? How long will it take us to get there?" She asked, putting her hand on his. "I would go to the ends of the earth to be with you, but it would be nice if it did not take us months to get there."

He chuckled. She did not know much of the world outside this village and, perhaps, the next. The expanse of the empire was great, but Rome itself should not take them more than a few weeks to get to. If they managed to secure horses it could cut their time in half and see them home before the end of the month.

"I will fine the quickest way to get us home. I give you my word."

"For that, and so much more, I will give you my heart." She said before pressing her lips to his once again.

The taste of her was bliss. She was like water to his parched soul and he wanted to drink her in until he drowned. There was no woman in his past who could possibly compare to this pale, fragile creature in his grasp. He had known women of the elite and he had known the daughters of the merchant guild and though they were lovely, passionate women, none of them stirred his heart or his loins as Tanaquil did. He wanted to explore her, body, and soul. Showing her the wonders of his world and learning everything that there was to learn about her. It would take a lifetime to learn it all and he was eagerly awaiting the chance to do so without the hindrance of bars between them.

"I will cherish you always. Once we are gone from here, the hunters far behind, I will make you my wife in the eyes of the law, your gods and my own."

"I would be honored to be your wife, Julius. It is a choice I make freely. Unlike the decision that my father will make for me if I stay here." Tanaquil said. "I must go back now, before someone comes looking for me. I fear that there would be violence brought against you if it were thought that you dared to break words with me without invitation."

"Little do they know that is the last thing upon my mind." Julius said with a smile he could not stop from spreading across his face. "The sweet thought of your lips against mine. The taste of your kiss will fill my dreams this night and every night from now until the end of time. Would there be violence if they knew that?"

"I think that the rage and violence would only be matched by the jealousy that they would feel if they were to know that the same thought floods my dreams as well. The desire for carnal knowledge of you, to be known fully by you, is inescapable for me." Tanaquil said, looking up through the inky black spikes of her lashes in a way that hinted at a deeper seduction than Julius had thought she was capable of.

"And do you wish to escape such thoughts Tanaquil?" He asked, holding her hand gently so that she could easily pull away and remove it.

"The only escape that is on my mind, Julius, is yours and the future for us that it will bring." She said.

Giving his hand a quick squeeze before stepping back from the bars he watched her sigh and wished that he could hold her tight against his chest. He wanted to be the one who calmed her troubles and soothed the worries that might plague her. Julius had never felt the urge to protect a specific woman before. There was the natural need to care for and protect all those in need of it, women, and children as well as the elderly, but this was different. He wanted to lay claim to her and make her concerns his own. Their bodies and souls would be one and the same went for their joys and sorrows.

"Then we should both put all our thoughts and energies towards achieving." He said with a nod. "I hope that Quellus will not press his case with your father too strongly. If he marries you before we can get away it will make him more determined to find us."

"Why would it make him more determined after the wedding than it will before?" She asked him, with a quick glance over her shoulder towards the feasting hut where noise was growing louder.

"There is no man alive that could have you and not chase the gods themselves to the edges of the earth to get you back in their arms if you were stolen away from them." Julius said, already feeling possessive of her. "I cannot and will not blame the man for all that he will do to try and get you back."

"Be careful what you say, Julius." Tanaquil said, quietly while she backed away. "The gods may hear you and choose to test us all against such a vow."

"I do not fear the gods." The centurion shook his head. "There is nothing that could do that would weaken my resolve in this."

Ch 6

The dawn came swiftly and yet Julius did not feel as weary as he had other mornings. The smile that Tanaquil had flashed towards him as she joined the other women on their way to the river to gather water for the day assured him that the words and the kiss from the night before were not a dream. She was going to not only help him to escape but join him as his wife as well. His life seemed to be moving from nightmare to his greatest dreams coming true. The only thing that was in his way was his captivity, and Quellus.

Today he would watch the guards and pay close attention to the keys and how they were fastened to the belt of his guards. He could not remove them himself, but he could give the information to Tanaquil so that she might use it and see them both to their freedom. She was bold, courageous, and clever. Julius knew that she would have no trouble using whatever information he could gather to make their escape easier to accomplish.

"Come, Roman dog." Quellus interrupted his thoughts of escape by smashing a stick against the bars. He unlocked the door and swung it open, the stick still in his hand like a sword.

Julius locked eyes with his jailor as he stepped out the door. There was a vicious mockery in the other man's eyes that gave Julius the feeling that he had something in mind that was as malicious as the man himself. He had almost passed Quellus when a movement out of the corner of the eye caught his attention and instinct kicked in.

He lifted an arm to block the blow and stepped back to avoid the blow of the stick. As much as Julius wanted to physically destroy Quellus he could not give any of the other guards more reason than they already had to become violent with him. He would not be able to run and take care of Tanaquil if he were injured in a fight today.

Quellus swung at him again and Julius simply stepped out of range. He wanted to taunt the man for a foolishly simply strategy. Even more, he desperately wanted to exert his own force in the situation. He knew that he needed to wait for the night of his escape when it would be useful as well as satisfying.

"You stand a coward, Roman dog." Quellus snarled when Julius blocked a third blow from the stick. "I thought Centurions were supposed to be warriors, not dancers."

"I can dance and kill you at the same time if that is what I wished to do." Julius said, catching hold of the stick. "I am not so foolish to think that I would not be struck down even in my moment of victory."

He used his hold on the stick to shove the other man backwards. As soon as he fell to the ground Julius released the weapon and held up his hands so that the other warriors that approached could see that he was not attempting to fight them all, merely defending himself against the unprovoked attack by one man.

They had him surrounded, their weapons brandished and rage in their eyes. It might not matter that he had not harmed their captain. They might kill him simply for refusing to take the beating that had obviously been intended for him.

Julius scanned the circle of men, calculating how he might take them down and how he could use their greater number to his advantage. It would not be easy, but it was possible that he could escape this with minor injuries. He would have tried it if he thought that there was chance he could escape with Tanaquil like this. There had not been time to prepare food or try to secure a horse that would be able to take them south fast enough that they would not be overtaken by these same men.

"I do not want to fight you." Julius said, holding up his palms. "I did not strike first. I only defended myself. I do not wish to fight."

"You are foolish to fight." One of the men said.

He was large and slow moving, but Julius thought that it was likely that he was one of those men that might take time to get moving but once he did then there was not much that would stop him. The others seemed to defer to the big man, since Quellus was still on the ground, so Julius addressed him calmly.

"I have no wish to fight. It is time to work, is it not?"

The large man looked him up and down while the other men readied themselves to attack on command. He looked down at Quellus and then back at Julius. They both knew that if there was a brawl Julius would die, but he would not be alone in death. With winter coming the tribe could hardly afford to lose their best warriors as well as the man they had enslaved for labour, which would certainly increase in the cold dark months ahead. They needed him to work and he needed to live. It was a simple and complimentary equation.

He just prayed that the other man saw it as well.

"Work. Yes." The man waved off the encircled men. "Today there will be work. Much work for you. You will do the workload of Quellus and your own work as well. Then nothing will be missed."

The group of men laughed and lowered their weapons. Julius realized that he may have won his battle for the day, but the war was still waging. True victory was still uncertain, and the battles were still screaming in his mind. There was a hope for victory now that had not been there yesterday though and he would cling to that. The thought of Tanaquil, her blush, her kiss, and her bravery in not only helping him to escape but joining him gave him drive and strength. He would not be broken, not today or any other day.

"Nothing will be missed. I will do the work." Julius said with a quick nod before he let himself be led off to the fields.

That day Julius worked harder than any other. He was sore from pulling the plow as well as the fight with Quellus but that was not going to stop him tonight. He knew that Tanaquil had hidden food sacks within the forest near the field and he was fairly certain that she was going to get the keys to his cell tonight and then they would secure a horse and make a run for Rome.

If they were blessed by the gods then the rest of the warriors would take his overplayed injuries as a sign that he was too weak to do anything except for sleep that night. They would never dream that he was not only plotting his escape but was physically capable of overpowering any of them if he needed to.

Freedom was so close Julius could almost taste it.

He watched Tanaquil walk across the clearing and wondered what she was going to taste like. He sat on the ground with the bread and water that was his evening meal and imagined her splayed out on the bed beneath him, naked and his to enjoy. She would give herself to him and he would do the same. There was no sweeter captivity than love and Julius was willing and eager to trade the freedom that he was about to risk his life for to have the chance to share that love with her. He was still surprised that she wanted the same. That she was willing to leave her life here to come back to Rome with him was a miracle.

It would also be a miracle if they were able to get to the capital. There was no doubt in his mind that the chief would send the best men that he had to bring his daughter back. They would be assuming that he had taken her as a prisoner, which would make them more dangerous. The fact that she was helping him would, he hoped, see their escape to some kind of advantage. He was not sure how yet, but when the time came Julius was sure that she would be as great an asset as she could.

The timing of the escape would be critical. Creating the illusion that he was exhausted and injured was the most important thing that he could do between that moment and the one where Tanaquil opened his cell door so that they could do their best to achieve mutual freedom. If their escape lasted only a few days, which he had to accept was a possibility, Julius began to consider the best way to spend the precious time that he would have with her. He pondered the kisses that they would share, the tender touches and the possible culmination of passion. It was a wonderful way to pass the hours waiting for her. He wondered if the taste of her lips would be like strawberries, if the nectar from her core would taste like honey or the juice of a ripe and luscious melon? How would their bodies fit together in the peak of their passionate joining?

The sun moved slowly towards the horizon but this time, instead of dreading the change of days he was having a hard time restraining his excitement. He wanted to be on his feet, pacing or exercising so that he was ready to run and ready to fight. If he did that it would attract the wrong kind of attention and he could not risk it, no matter how important it was. Julius looked to the heavens and prayed that the gods would see fit to bless their escape with ease and darkness to cover the act.

"If you see me free of this place while I still live I swear to you that I will never name any man, woman or child a slave of my house. I will do all that I can to ease the lives of the slaves that I come to know and I will never forget the sting of the rod in the hand of a man that feels he is my master."

There was no way to tell if they heard him or if the gods of this foreign land would grant the petition of a man who had been intent upon conquering it and all it's people. Julius knew that he simply had to have faith and do all that he could to earn it for himself and Tanaquil. The gods would grant his request, or they would not. He would honor his vow regardless and never, ever, own a slave again. He might pay an honest wage to those he set free, but he would never hold the title of Dominus over any being once he was free. He could not put another soul through this kind of agony. No man with a soul who lived through captivity could.

The sunset came and it was glorious. Red and orange with a soft pink edge that faded into the deep dark that crept slowly towards the horizon. So soon now. It would not take long for the village to quiet down and for all the occupants to find themselves in bed for the night. Then their quest for freedom would begin.

It was so close now Julius could taste it.

He lay on his side, watching as each home went dark and listening to the growing silence. It was a beautiful sound. It seemed almost loud when Tanaquil whispered his name from the darkness on the other side of the bars.

"Julius? Julius it is time." She whispered. "We have to go now."

"I am ready. You have secured the key?" He asked, rising slowly from the ground where he had been laying.

She held up the key and flashed him a smile.

"Be quick and be silent." She whispered, turning the key in the lock. Looking around to check for anyone watching them Tanaquil opened the door for him "Be free."

Ch 7

Julius stepped out of the cell and into the village square. Despite having done so for weeks on end this felt somehow different, significant. The weight of drudgery was gone from his shoulders and there was a surety in his step that he had not thought would return but it grew with each step away from his confinement. He could feel his confidence returning and if there had been a sword in his hand he would have swung in an arch to remind himself of the deadly skills he possessed. That would have to wait though. He possessed nothing for a weapon, yet, not even a stick.

"We must lock the door and then go. We do not have much time and we are far from free of the reach of this place yet." Tanaquil pulled him from his thoughts and back to the present.

"Of course. Throw the keys into the cell. They will not think to look for them there. If they are seen then they will not be able to get to them without destroying the whole cell." Julius grinned.

Tanaquil managed to land the keys close to the center of the cell, under the small stool so that they would be harder to see and even harder to retrieve.

"Now we will go." She said, taking his hand. "I will guide us through the forest and to the river beyond it. You will need lead from there for that is all the land that I know."

He was amazed that her exposure to the world was so restrained, so limited. Perhaps the city of Rome would be too overwhelming for her? One of the smaller communities might be easier for her to adjust to. He would find a town with an arena and gladiators that he could guard and easily maintain a house for his new wife, where no one would ask questions.

It did not take long to get through the trees, even though they had to stop twice. Once because he fell, tripping on a branch as he tried to keep up to Tanaquil's speed through the brush and the second was when she gestured for a stop so that they could listen for any sounds that the escape had been discovered. There had been no alarm raised yet. If the gods were with them they would reach the river within the hour and by the time the sky was lit by the dawn they might be far enough away to risk sleeping in shifts for a few hours before they continued.

Julius did not like it but there was the probability that he would need to rob someone for coin or steal a horse so that they could get as far away as soon as possible. He hated to expose Tanaquil to the violence that came with what he had to do, but he would do so if he needed to. Once they found a horse it would be simple and a fast escape. Until they were at least three days away he would not stop looking over his shoulder to make sure that they were not being followed.

Tanaquil might think that Quellus would not follow them that far but Julius knew that the man was more possessive than she might think he was. A man who saw women as a possession, not a person, would not stop hunting for her if he thought she ha been stolen from him. There would be a confrontation between them before this was over and it would be deadly. The longer that Julius could delay that confrontation the better his own chances for survival were.

"Just over that ridge is the bank of the river." Tanaquil said, pointing to the edge of the forest. "This is as far as I know."

"I will take the lead from here." Julius said, running his hand down her arm to take her hand. "Though there is something that I need to do before that."

"Oh, of course. I did not give you time before we ran." She turned her back to him.

Confused he stared at her back for a moment before he realized that she thought he needed to relieve himself and was having the grace to give him a moment of privacy.

"No, dear woman." He said, taking her by the shoulder and turning her to face him. "I had no chance to kiss my future bride."

Even in the dark of the forest Julius could see the way Tanaquil's face lit up. She had not thought that he had meant his words of desire and devotion for her. How better to demonstrate to her that he meant what he said about building a life with her than to show her, physically, what she meant to him.

He pulled her into his arms, slowly encircling her shoulders to hold her against his chest. It felt so good to have her warm against his skin, his hand running smoothing up and down her back before he cupped her cheek and tilted her face upwards.

"A bride deserves to be kissed, especially one so brave." He kissed her right cheek.

"One so strong." He kissed her left cheek. "One so amazing as you."

His lips touched hers and it was like fire flowed from her into the kiss and into his blood. He had meant to be soft and tender but instead he had to fight for control of himself. With no bars between them Julius' hands could explore and caress his woman in ways that he never had before. The fullness of her curves fit into his hands while hers danced elegantly up his back and into his hair. There was no more pretext of the shy and demure village girl now. She was a fully blossomed woman in his arms and as soon as it was safe there would be nothing in the world that would stop him from joining with her in an embrace so full of passion the gods would stop in the heavens to observe their mortal divinity.

"Julius."

His name whispered on her lips was one of the most beautiful things he had ever heard. Her fingers threaded into his hair and pulled his head down so that she could deepen the kiss with a sweep of her tongue against his. It was a heaven he could not have imagined. If there had not been a chance that they would be caught he would have taken her against the tree. Even with the threat hanging over them it was temping.

So very tempting.

"Tanaquil. I want you now. I know we do not have much time, but do you want this now? It will not be romantic, and it will not be slow. It will be raw and passionate. It will be real." He said, his voice hoarse with desire.

Her body pressed against him was agony and bliss bound together. It was hard to hold back, but he would never push, never force. He did consider begging though. The words were almost at his lips when she whispered breathlessly to him.

"Take me now. With the gods to stand as witnesses there is no man upon the earth that can undo such a thing."

Her hand caressed his cheek then down his arm to take hold of his hand and press his palm against her breast.

"Make me your wife, Julius. Here, before any man might stop us. It cannot be undone."

He pressed a kiss to her lips and kneaded the soft flesh in his grasp until she was moaning against his lips. A few careful steps took them to the thick trunk of a tree, and he lifted Tanaquil to wrap her legs around him while resting her back against the support. She pulled her dress from her shoulders while he slid his hand between her thighs to stroke the entrance to her core.

When his fingers grew slick with her arousal Julius could not help but to taste the sample of her sweetness. More glorious than he had hoped, she was a sweet elixir on his tongue. Another night he would dine on her until she shattered in his arms. Her body would buck and bend in response to his touch that night. Tonight, it would be a passionate, penetrative, claiming that neither god nor man could ever deny or put aside.

Tanaquil was writhing against his chest, the tips of her fingers scratching his back as she begged him for more. He returned his fingers to her entrance and slid two inside her. Julius watched her head roll back as she inhaled sharply. He pressed his thumb against her while pumping his fingers into her while she rode his hand with wild abandon, using his shoulders to leverage her body harder and faster on his fingers.

She was gloriously passionate, sensuously wild and when he locked his eyes to hers he knew that there was never going to be another woman in his life like her. He would never need a lover the way that some married men did. This wonderful creature in his arms would be all he ever needed.

"Are you ready for me?" He asked, kissing her lips firmly as he withdrew his hand. His cock was hard as steel and the moisture at his tip was begging to join with her.

"Yes, my Roman. Fill me, have me, take me and make me yours alone." She said breathlessly, opening her eyes to meet his gaze. "I want you."

Their eyes stayed locked to each other as he reached to adjust himself at her entrance. Slowly he eased her downwards. A hiss escaped his clenched teeth when his tip pierced her core. She was slick with arousal and her heat welcomed him with ease. Slowly Julius built a rhythm of thrusts into her, allowing them both to grow accustomed to each other.

Once he had worked his length inside her Julius paused, letting her rest while his hands held her in place. He kissed her deeply, sweeping his tongue against hers until she buried her fingers in his hair to pull him closer.

"Ready?" He asked her softly, moving his lips to kiss her neck and lick the beating pulse at it's base.

She nodded and began to rock her hips, pumping him in and out of her while he braced a hand on the trunk of the tree. She felt exquisite and her soft moans that accompanied her breathy gasps told him that she felt the same about him. Together they began to move faster, more frantically, and Julius had to lift Tanaquil from resting against the trunk of the tree so that he could put his own against it to keep her from hurting herself. She continued to ride him passionately. Her hands clenched tight on his shoulders for leverage and one of his hands gripping her hip to help build the friction and sensation growing at the base of his spine.

"More." She whispered in his ear, grinding down on his shaft. "Harder."

Julius smiled and kissed her firmly on the lips. If she wanted more then he would give it to her. Altering the angle of his hips he was able to put more power into his thrusts and meet her need with equal force. It only took moments for her to be tight around him with her hands gripping tight to his arms so that she did not fall. He watched as her eyes closed, knowing that her release would soon come. He was ready for her, trying to hold himself back so that they could reach those heights together.

"Julius, oh gods. Yes."

Tanaquil cried, arching her back so sharply that he thought she might break in half. He felt her tighten around him, squeezing hard. With a groan he thundered his hips against her until he spilled his seed deep within her core. He wanted to roar his pleasure like a wild animal, tell all the world that she was his, but that would most assuredly alert anyone hunting them to the direction that they had run.

For tonight he would have to settle for gently setting his woman on her feet, embracing her against his chest so that she could hear the beating of his heart while he kissed her forehead and stroked her hair.

"You are so incredible, my Tanaquil. You are the light of my life and my hero." He said softly. "I wish that we could rest, but we must make haste under the cover of darkness and get as far from the village as we can before the light of day forces us to hide. That is when we will be able to rest."

"Lead the way and I will follow, Centurion." She replied with a smile.

"Then come, we should go now to the water." Julius said, taking her hand and starting off towards the soft sound of the river.

Ch 8

The rest of the night had been spent crossing the river and making it look as though they had fled upstream before using the water to move downstream as far as they could stand being in the cold water in the dark of night. Julius did not want his new wife to become ill on the journey to Rome but there was no better way to get far from the search party in mere hours than the risk the water.

The sun had begun to tease the horizon and Julius was doing his best to find or build shelter so that they could sleep for a few hours without the worry of discovery. He was fairly certain that they had evaded the hunters for the time being. It would not take them long to discover that the trail that they had made in the sand led to nowhere. They would come looking soon and Julius knew that he had to get Tanaquil as far away as possible.

They were lucky to find a grove of trees not far from the river. There were enough branches that were broken from the trunks that Julius was able to build a shelter low to the ground that would hide them from the light of the sun as well as all but the most careful hunters. They might find the escapees, it was possible, but this was as far as they could go without sleep. The chance had to be taken and they would deal with whatever waited for them afterwards.

Julius tucked Tanaquil to the back of the low-lying shelter. She was nearly asleep as soon as she laid down, her back to the outside and her sweet face inwards towards him. He rested his head upon his arm, a smile on his face despite the danger that chasing them. Even if the rest of their lives were spent running, watching over their shoulders, as long as he was permitted to fall asleep each night looking at her cherubic face then he would be a happy man. He reached out his hand to caress the soft pillow of her cheek and closed his eyes to drift off to sleep.

His dreams were filled of hopes for the future that they would build together. His parents would adore her. When they had children, making their family even bigger, then they would know that the gods blessed them. Julius knew that his joy would be complete the day he held his child in his arms. He was not a man that cared if it was a boy or girl that he was blessed with first. He knew that many men had a preference. A son could carry on the bloodline while a daughter could bring alliances with prosperous partners. All he wanted was a child to love and to be the blending of himself and Tanaquil.

His hand slid down her arm so that the tips of his fingers could touch her stomach.

Perhaps they would be blessed soon, and their joining would be complete. They would be bound in blood. The thought was pleasing and one that he would bring into conversation later that day when they were on their escape once again. Her face would surely light up with joy when she heard his plans, his hopes for their future together. That image, her warm and bright smile, was what guided him to sleep.

Julius did not know how many hours had passed before he woke but when he did Tanaquil was watching him, resting her head on her hand.

"Did you dream sweetly my husband? There has been a smile upon your face since before I woke to see it." She said before she leaned down to kiss him softly on the lips. "It is past midday now. We should eat before we leave the shelter to the trees."

"I dreamed of your smile and that of our children so there is no doubt that I had a smile upon my own face for such a sight would be the purest of joys." Julius said, sitting up and taking the bowl of river water that she offered him to drink.

"Our children? It warms my heart that such a thought is in your mind as well." Tanaquil said, touching his hand.

"I do not wish to linger here for long." He said, looking back in the direction that they had come from. "It will not take them long to discover that we did not go to the north. They will come this way soon and if they have horses it will be even quicker than we have accounted for."

"You still need to eat, Julius, or their victory will be all but assured if they do find us." She countered, handing him a portion of meat and cheese as well as bread. "So, you will eat and then we will hide any proof of our stay here. Then we will depart as quickly as possible and get as far from here as we can."

He took a bite and chuckled. She was a wise woman with a steady determination that he needed in his life. She would be the kind of wife that managed him as well as she would manage their household. That was a strangely satisfying thought, one that he never thought that he would have. He enjoyed it nonetheless and with a wicked grin he asked.

"Does my clever wife have a plan in mind for that leg of the journey as well? Perhaps I shall let you be our guide. I will happily play the dim-witted Roman servant to your wisewoman of Gaul."

"You stand a servant to no man or woman Julius Lucius. I know that you jest though I would remind you that I am no fearful child." Tanaquil said with a confident smile. "If you put a weapon in my hand I may not know how to use it, but I will not be afraid to try."

She said it with such a certainty, a confidence, that Julius could not doubt her sincerity. It would not be a bad idea to try and find her a weapon of her own on the way to the Republic. The women of Rome may not often carry weapons, they considered themselves too proper for such barbarity. They would certainly respect Tanaquil for being skilled with the same weapons that the female gladiators, the gladiatrix, used in the arena. If they were going to call her a savage then he should do whatever he could to make sure that it was a word said in awe and not condescending condemnation.

"I believe you. You might strike fear and awe into the proper Roman matrons. A sight that I long to see almost as strongly as I wish to see the walls of Rome itself." Julius said, rising to his feet and holding out a hand to his wife to help her to rise. "We should start the journey again. Some weapons and perhaps a horse if one can be found will be my priority if we find a town or a farm."

"I think that speed should be our greater concern, Julius. If we try to buy weapons or steal them, it will be remembered much more clearly than if we simply pass through the towns as quickly as possible. We should try to be forgettable." Tanaquil said as Julius led her towards the road.

"I do not think that is possible. In the absence of being forgotten we must be far from here by the time that someone arrives to ask about us." He said firmly.

She would think that he was attempting to flatter her if he said that her beauty was the kind that a man would remember and, truthfully, that was only part of the dilemma. He was a Roman and even without his armor it was obvious that he was a trained soldier. The farmers and craftsmen of the small Gaulish towns would know that he was different than they were. Coupled with Tanaquil's beauty there was little chance that they would not be remembered, especially if Quellus or any of the hunters asked for a couple that matched their exact description.

"Will you allow me to take the bag of supplies?" Julius asked after a few minutes of silence. They might disagree on the tactics of their escape but regardless of that fact he was a good man and wanted to take of his wife. "I should have taken it last night when we left. Apologies."

He held out his hand to take the bag but was confused when she paused, holding tight to the bag over her shoulder. It looked heavier and bulkier than he estimated it should be with only food inside it. Why would she not let him carry the weight for her?

Of course.

She had likely taken a few trinkets, things of emotional consequence and was worried that he would disapprove since their ability to move swiftly might be hampered by the extra weight in the bag.

"What is it that you have brought that you do not want me to see?" Julius asked with a smile. He would have to work on her expectation that he would be as heavy handed as her father was. "I can understand that you needed to bring things from your home that hold value to you, but you do not need to carry them on your back while I am here."

"The burden is not just my simple treasures. Those are few and light. I did not think that you would object to them." Tanaquil said, setting the bag on the ground. "The bulk, the weight, is what I took for you so that you need not return home in disgrace."

"Took for me?" Julius reached for the bag. "What did you take Tanaquil?"

His mind spun with thoughts of what she could have done. She was obviously worried that he would disapprove. He prayed that she had not taken something sacred. Though that would make his return to Rome look more like a victory than an escape it would also increase the rage and determination of those that followed them.

The weight of the bag was more significant than he had expected. The fact that she had carried it so far and had made no mention of that was as impressive as it was worrisome. She must have truly been concerned about his reaction to what it held.

He sifted carefully past the food, reaching for the heavy object at the bottom. When his hand touched something familiar he looked up at her and smiled. It was better than he had hoped. He slid his fingers around the cool ivory they knew well and drew the object out of the bag.

His soldiers pugio rested in his hand, the steel shining in the bright light of the sun when he drew it from its sheath. He remembered the day that he had first held it when he received his armor and began training in the legions. It had been personally presented to him by his hero, Titus Claudius, who was no longer serving but had become one of the wealthiest men in the Republic. It was a day that he would never forget, just as this one was.

"Why? Why would you hide this from me thinking that I would be displeased?" He asked, placing a kiss on the top of her head. "This is a wonderful tool and might be the difference between the success and failure of our venture."

"I was worried that if I gave it to you in the village that you would use it there. I chose you. I still choose you, but I do not wish to see the blood of those I love shed upon the ground so that I may pursue my heart. It would have been too much to bear." She said slowly. "I meant to keep it as a surprise once we were closer to the Republic of Rome, when we might meet with the legions and the need to prove your identity became imminent. The more you spoke of needing a weapon, as well as a horse, the more I came to realize that it could not wait."

"Tanaquil, thank you for this. Please know that I would never shed the blood of your kinsmen without the greatest of need." Julius took her hand in his after he fastened the knife to his belt. "I know that what you have chosen is not easy and there will be days where you might hold regret. I can only hope that the days where you are happy will outnumber those of regret. I swear to you that I will never stop making your happiness the first priority of my day and the last concern of my night. We will face troubles in our future, but we will face them together."

"Then, my centurion." She said, kissing his cheek. "Let us carry on towards that future and hope that our greatest troubles come many years from now."

Ch 9

It was late in the afternoon when they reached a village that had stone buildings. One of these, Julius was relived to discover, had rooms that were available for a few coins. Even better was that Tanaquil had been clever enough to bring the coin purse from his things that her father had taken from him. There was no need to barter away his weapon to get a warm bath and a good night sleep, in a bed instead of the ground. He could give Tanaquil a night like she had never had before, a proper wedding night. It would be a wonderful night to remember as the start of their lives together and the first of many gifts that he would give to her in their life together.

"Oh Julius. I have never seen such rooms before." Tanaquil said, making the Centurion smile.

If this was her idea of finery then the splendor of Rome might overwhelm her completely. He could almost picture her face when they arrived. Her eyes would light up and she would smile as she stared at the wonders of the great city. There would be so much to show her and to share with her.

"My dear wife, these pale in comparison to those that wait for us upon our return. I am glad though, that it does not take all the grandness and luxury of Rome to impress you for it would be beyond my means to provide." Julius said, sliding his arms around her and drawing his wife close to press against him.

"Let us bathe, eat and rest. The days to come will be the hardest but when we reach the coast I certain that we will be able to barter passage on a ship to take us to the Republic and then we will be no more than a day or two from my home. From our home."

She turned around to face him and wrapped her arms around his neck.

"That sounds like it will be wonderful. An adventure unlike anything I have ever dreamed of."

She reached up to kiss his lips, which then spread in a smile as he stroked her face with the back of his fingers.

"It will be the first of many, my dear wife. I want to give you adventures, show you incredible sights that you have never dreamed possible before. Tanaquil, I want to show you my world."

"Then we should bathe so that we can greet those adventures without the smell of the wild upon us." She replied, stepping back from his hold but keeping his hand in hers. "The inn keepers wife told me that there are scented oils for the bath. I would see them well used so that you do not bring the smell of the past to our bed tonight."

"Then I shall let you choose the scent from what they have. I would do anything that is within my power to make this night everything that it should be, everything that you have dreamed it could be."

Julius watched his wife practically run to the room where the hot bath had been drawn for them. Such a small thing, so simple that it had never crossed his mind, and it brought her so much joy.

The small room was filled with steam when he stepped through the heavy curtains that had been hung for privacy. Tanaquil was standing at the table smelling the different oils excitedly with a cloth wrapped around her curves. Her eyes closed as she inhaled each different scent. Stripping off his clothes so that they could be washed Julius watched his woman experience the exotic scents before adding one to the water. When she stepped into the warmth he watched her entire body quiver with excitement,

"Go all the way in. Dip under the edge and feel the heat of it washing over you. Tanaquil, you will love it and I will love watching you." He said with a smile.

It was so wonderful to watch her in the water. Every curve was softened and accentuated by the ripples and her face was the picture of delight. He had never thought to consider that she had likely never bathed in anything other than the river and it was even less probable that she had ever had a bath that was steaming hot. For a moment she looked as though she was afraid she might cook in the heat, so he joined her and pressed a kiss to her bare shoulder.

"It is wonderful, is it not?" He asked, spinning her on her toes in the water.

"It is a marvel. I never thought something like bathing could feel so wonderful, so warm. I could stay here all night and be happy." She said in reply.

"When we have our house in the Republic you will be able to take a bath just like this whenever it pleases you to do so." He dipped beneath the water and pulled her down with him. When they came back up he drew her against his chest, felt her nipples pearl and lowered his head to kiss her with all the passion of a man set free.

"Do proper Roman husbands and wives take their pleasure with each other in bathes like this?" Tanaquil asked while her hand slid from his shoulder down beneath the water.

When she took his hardened shaft in her grasp and stroked him from the base up to the tip then back down Julius could not hold back the tremor of delight that she was so bold and full of desire. Her touch along with the steam and the heat of the water brought him to the height of arousal. He wanted to lift her onto the edge of the tub so that he could lower her core onto his cock and use their bodies to make waves of water to match the rising tide of their desire. They would flood each other's senses, and the floor, before they were finished.

"Men and women of Rome take their pleasure when and where they are able, whether it is proper or not could be debated by those much wiser than myself. One of the many things that I have learned while I have been here as a captive among your people is that propriety pales in comparison to passion, freedom and love, even if is newly burst into bloom."

"You learned that from my people?" She said, kissing his chest tenderly. "What other lessons did you learn? What skills do you have from Rome to teach me?"

Julius chuckled and traced his palms down her sides to grip her hips. He pulled her towards him as he leaned back against the side of the tub.

"There are many skills from Rome that I could teach you. That I will teach you over time." He said, nuzzling her neck. "I think that the first thing we should review is kissing. Kissing is particularly important you know."

"Is it? I had no idea." Was Tanaquil's coy reply.

He loved that she was playful as well as passionate.

When she leaned up to kiss him Julius inhaled sharply when her nipples, tightened to buds by the air above the water, pressed into his chest. The friction of the connection sent a fresh bolt of desire through him and a groan escaped his lips. The sound of his desire was echoed by the woman in his arms as she pressed a hot kiss at the base of his throat.

"They kiss in many places, the people of Rome." He said, kissing her lips, her cheek, her throat. "Where do you want to kiss me Tanaquil?"

"I want to kiss you here." She touched his neck with her fingertip before pressing her lips to his pulse.

"Also, here." She said, kissing his nipple.

"Those both feel good. Where else do you want to kiss me?"

He wanted to laugh at the simplicity of kisses, the seriousness in her eyes stopped him. This was important to her in ways that he had not considered. Julius had not asked her if she had been intimate with a man before or what she like and desired. While she studied his body to find the answer to his question he searched her face trying to guess what she would do next, where she would want to touch next.

He was holding back his own urge to take charge of the situation, to lead her towards deeper passion. That was not going to help him accomplish what he wanted though. He could not learn about Tanaquil if he were always in control. Every time that she chose freely it revealed something else about her that he wanted to study and understand. Her world was so different than his had ever been in his lifetime and he wanted to know everything that he could about her. For a woman from a culture that his peers would describe as savage and primitive his wife had an elegance and grace that was rare in Rome.

"I want to kiss you here." She said, taking his cock in her grasp. "Sit upon the edge of the water please."

He was amazed and thrilled.

While he complied with her command Julius stroked a hand through her hair, the long, wet strands tangled around his fingers, but he was careful not to pull her towards his erection. He did not want her to think that he was going to force her to do anything that she was not completely prepared for.

The first touch of her tongue to his flesh felt shy, tentative. The tremble in her breath against his skin told Julius that she was as nervous as she was curious. His lovely, confident bride moving her lips up and down his cock was a more beautiful sight than he could have imagined. Her mouth was delivering a perfect pressure, a suction that was powerful, sexual, and driving him wild. Julius' hands were gripping the edge of the tub so hard he thought he might crack the marble.

"That is a kiss worthy of Olympus itself, Tanaquil. I will give you the same kiss soon so that you can know what is to rise to the heavens with the touch of only lips." He said between clenched teeth as he cast his eyes up to the ceiling and prayed for self control. "Tonight, in this moment, I want more than just kisses."

Lowering his eyes to lock with hers Julius watched as Tanaquil stood, rising out to the water like a nymph from the myths.

"What else do you want Julius? What more shall we share this night together, our first in a bed?" She asked him, running her palms up his thighs while her green eyes sparked at him. "What do you want to do with me?"

"Everything." Was the only thing he could think to say in response.

Julius slid his hands over the curve of Tanaquil's backside, lower until the tips of his fingers were dancing across the back of her thighs. He lifted her out of the water and guided her legs around his waist. He could feel the heat of her core pressing against his erection and could not contain the hungry growl that escaped him as he dragged his teeth across the ridge of her collarbone.

"You want me Centurion? To bury yourself inside me?" She moaned in his ear. "Right here on the side of the bath?"

"I would take you anywhere I could. Anywhere you would allow me too I would be with you." Julius said, his voice rasping against her skin.

She was rocking her hips gliding up and down his cock with the slickness of her increasing arousal in imitation of the act they would begin momentarily. As soon as he was outside of his mind with the need for her and she had worked herself into a frenzy of need that could not be contained.

"What if the innkeeper and his wife were to see us?" Tanaquil asked, gripping his shoulders to leverage her motions nearly the entire length of his shaft.

"I do not care if the gods themselves paused to observe every thrust I made I would still want to fill you completely and take us both the edge of our sanity, of our passion sharp as a knife."

He held his breath when she paused at the crest of her erotic temptation. When she brushed back the hair that had fallen into his eyes Julius turned his head to nip at her wrist.

"And I would take us over that edge into ecstasy and bliss." She whispered hotly in his ear before easing the head of his cock to her entrance and slowly sliding down his length.

The slow build of pressure as her heat surrounded him was exquisite, as was her gasp when she had sheathed herself fully. Slowly she began to rise and descend using his shoulders for leverage until Julius gripped her hips. Locking their eyes, he began to increase the pace, grinning when she raised her hands into her hair, thrusting her beautiful breasts towards his mouth.

Leaning backwards to lay on the cool stone floor Julius could not help but enjoy the view as her body moved. Palming a breast with one hand and gripping her hip with the other Julius surrendered to the uninhibited moment and let his wife ride herself to orgasm with a shattering cry that he echoed moments later then gathered her to his chest with a loving kiss to the top of her hair.

"My beautiful wife. Let us enjoy the bath for a few moments more and then I shall show you how Romans make love in a bed."

Ch 10

Their night had been filled with passion followed by the deepest rest that Julius could remember. Waking up with Tanaquil in his arms had been the most wonderful dawn of his life and he could not wait until it was like that every morning of their lives. He tightened his hold on her for a moment, pulling his wife against his chest before he placed a kiss at the nape of her neck.

"My beloved, it is time to wake. We must carry on with our journey and keep far enough ahead of Quellus and the other hunters that we can escape on the coast. One day more, maybe two, and we will be free from the risk of capture."

He hated to leave the bed and even more he hated to pull her from it instead of joining her to make passionate love again as they had the previous night when they had left the bath and come to the room that had been prepared for them. The innkeeper's wife had been a kind and romantic woman who had understood the significance of the night and had done her best to make everything as perfect as was possible. Julius wished that he had more coins that he could give to thank her for what she had done but they would be needed to secure the passage back to the Republic and so his sincere thanks would have to do.

"I am reluctant to leave such luxury, husband." Tanaquil said, stretching beneath the covers and then sitting up. "Even knowing that the sooner we return to your home the sooner that this will be our life every morning. This moment seems to be perfect to me."

The blanket fell from her body like the water had in the bath and revealed the rounded curve of what Julius considered to be the most beautiful breasts in all the world. His mouth watered at the sight and he had to force himself to stick to his resolution that they depart within the hour.

"I do not wish to leave it either my dearest heart. If time were of no concern I would happily keep you in this bed for days unending." Julius kissed her quickly then began to dress. "I may yet consider that to be necessary once we are settled in our new home. For that to come to pass we must complete our mission, which also means that we must leave within the hour."

"Will you promise that we will find a bed such as this again as soon as we are able?" She asked him, sliding out from beneath the rest of the covers to dress beside him. "I think that there are many more ways to make love to you, that would be made more comfortable, with the use of a bed like this."

Julius laughed, fastened the notch in his belt and kissed her on the tip of her nose.

"If that is my wife's desire than I shall see to it that her wish is done with as much speed as can be summoned."

"Then you will find your wife a happy woman indeed, Centurion." Tanaquil replied, cupping his cheek, and pulling him down for another, deeper, kiss. "Though I stand happier now than I ever thought to be in my life."

"Of that I am glad. I do not know if I shall ever recover from the honor that you have bestowed upon me by choosing me. I swear that I will spend the rest of my days doing my best to be worthy of you and your love." Julius said, taking her hands in his and kissing her once more before lifting the bag of their belonging and leading her towards the door.

Before he had the chance to open it Julius was surprised to when it was pushed open by the wife of the innkeeper. Her face was flushed, and she was struggling to catch her breath as though she had been running and she was wringing her hands with great agitation. Her tone was full of concern when she found her voice.

"You must not go down there. The danger is too great. There are men with weapons that are looking for you both. I think that they mean to do you great harm."

Julius reached for the blade that he had secured to his belt and attempted to step around the woman. Her hands and those of his wife reached to stop him from crossing the threshold and heading to face their pursuers.

"Julius you cannot fight them alone. We must hide or run." Tanaquil said quietly. "I know that it is not in your nature to do either of those. I hate to ask it of you, but I would rather you live to see our return to your homeland than see how many of them you are capable of killing before you are struck down yourself."

"Listen to your wife, Roman, and do not make her a widow so young or so needlessly." The older woman said, moving to stand in front of him. "There is another way to get you both away from here without them seeing you."

"You know that I am a man of Rome and yet you take risks to help me? Why?" Julius asked, releasing his hold on the weapon.

"Do not mistake me. I have no love for your people or their attempt to conquer all the world. The way that you love your wife, treating her with such tenderness and respect, earned the respect of my husband and myself. There are some things that can overcome barriers and love is one of them." She smiled at them both and opened the door to lead them to their escape.

Julius made sure that Tanaquil was between himself and their guide so that if the trackers came upon them it would be him and not his wife that was the first to be attacked. He would not put it above Quellus to be the kind of man that would stab his enemy in the back, and he did not want it to be Tanaquil or the kind woman who was helping them to escape who suffered the injury. He prayed that neither the woman or her husband came to any harm for helping them. There were not many people in the world that would have helped them, and he would hate to think that such rare souls suffered pain for their kindness.

"If you are careful and quiet you can climb onto the roof of the next villa. They have stairs on the far side that you could use to get down and escape the town before you are discovered." She said with a smile, handing Tanaquil a scarf for her head. "Use this so that they do not see your hair. Such a colour is hard to forget."

"Gratitude, good woman." Julius said, taking her hand and kissing the backs of her fingers. "I pray that the gods bless you for your kindness and that no harm comes to you because of your aid."

"They would be fools indeed if they made such an attempt." She said with a smile. "I will pray that the two of you are able to make your escape and find out if this love of yours can stand the test of time. Go with blessings behind you."

They made their way carefully out onto the roof, trying not to slip or make a noise. The voices of the trackers were easily heard through the windows and Julius watched as Tanaquil grew more and more visibly nervous. He was worried that she might faint or make some sound that would alert those below to the escape that they were trying to make.

"Careful." He whispered, taking her hand once they got to the edge of the roof.

They could not climb to the next roof. The divide was too great for anything but a running leap. The jump would not be hard for him but there was no way that Tanaquil could accomplish it without a run that was too dangerous on the roof. He would have to lift her up and toss her as carefully as possible. Julius knew that the noise from her landing would be the end of their hiding. They would be discovered. Speed, luck, and a few places to hide would be their only chance to escape after this. There was no other choice but to try. If they ran they might be caught and have to fight, Julius had no intention of going back to captivity, but they might succeed in escaping. If they stayed they would be certainly be caught and those that helped them might face harm for helping them. The next roof over was the only chance they had at freedom together.

"I will have to toss you. Will you be able to make it without crying out? I promise that you will make the distance so there is no fear that you will fall." He whispered in her ear.

"The noise will alert them to our location. Julius we cannot risk that with you on this side of the divide. If they catch you, they will kill you without pause. My father will have told them to bring me home alive. You must jump first."

She was right, of course she was right, and he hated it.

The first thing he would do in their position would be to kill the man that had taken a woman captive and ran away with her. Now that they were this close to being captured, her people closing in on them with every step, it would not be his strength that would save them, but the love and loyalty of the enemy.

"I will not leave you behind. You are my wife." Julius said, brushing her cheek with his fingers. "I will catch you when you leap. I will always catch you."

She nodded. The smile that had begun on her lips quickly faded when the sound of footsteps sounded on the stairs behind them.

"Julius go." She said, looking over her shoulder then back to him. "You must leap now, or all is lost."

Julius nodded and kissed her. It was firm, brief, full of the words there was no time to say, then he took a few steps backwards and made a run for the divide between the buildings. He vaulted through the air and landed on the other rooftop, tucked in his shoulder so that he rolled to a stop instead of sliding. Jumping to his feet the joyful roar of success died on his lips when he saw the trackers surrounding Tanaquil and Quellus standing with a bow aiming straight at him.

"We find you at last, Roman." Quellus said. "Last for you at least."

The arrogance in his voice was like sand in a wound and Julius' fists clenched instinctively. More than almost anything he wanted to fight this man, a fair fight to the end this time. There was no chance that Quellus was going to be willing to wager the success of his mission on a fight he had nearly lost once already.

"You will not hurt my wife." Julius said, inwardly reveling in the shock on the face of each man when they realized that he had not kidnapped her but that they had run away together. "We are going to Rome, together."

"Wife? You dared to force the daughter of our chief, destined to be high priestess, to be the serving wife to a Roman dog? You defiled her?" Quellus said, drawing the bow string tight.

He was ready to fire, which meant that he was on the edge of losing his control. This was the moment, when his emotions were high, that Julius could try to get through to him.

"I did not know that was her future. I was simply honored that she agreed to be my wife. I had no need to force anything, unlike you, Quellus." Julius said, looking at Tanaquil. "I want to spend my life making her happy. Do you not want that for her? Or is your need to possess her so great that you would condemn her to a life of misery just so that you could treat her like a treasured possession?"

The string of the bow relaxed as the man considered the accusation. Julius let his eyes lock with those of his wife once more. He drank in her beauty in case this was, in fact, the last moments that they had in this life. He would wait for her. In this life or the next, there would be no one else in his heart but her. All of the words that he had not yet said to her were sitting like stones in his gut.

What would Quellus do?

"You are a fool, Roman, and she is a greater one still." One of the other men said. "By mistake you have defiled the body of a priestess for which the gods will choose your punishment. She knew her destiny, she took the vows to withhold her body from the touch of any man. The breaking of those vows carries a sentence of death."

He drew a blade from his belt and lunged towards Tanaquil despite the blended voice of Julius and Quellus crying together.

"NO!"

Ch 11

Julius rushed to the edge of the roof and Quellus dropped his bow. The man with the knife looked back and forth between the two warriors. Julius could see the panic in his eyes, but more than the pity he would usually feel for a man who was that afraid the centurion wished that he could rip that blade from his hand and bury it in his throat. Any man who dared to touch his wife, let alone threaten her life simply for loving him, deserved to die.

Slowly and painfully.

Apparently it was something, the only thing, that he and Quellus agreed on. Even though there was another bow aimed at Julius now, the one that had been in the hands of the tracker now lay on the tiles of the roof. The Centurion had to stand and watch his enemy attempt to save the life of the woman he loved.

"No one needs to know, Lasar. No one needs to know what happened before we arrived." Quellus said, stepping towards them. "We can kill the Roman and then no one will know that we did not get here in time. You do not want to kill Tanaquil. We have called each other friends all of our lives. That does not have to end now."

The man, Lasar, started to lower the knife from Tanaquil's throat and Julius let out the breath that he had been holding. He would deal with their attempt to kill him and take his wife back to the village once there was not a blade at her throat and an arrow pointed at his chest. This was the time for calm, rational thoughts, and actions, not heroics.

"No. I do not wish to take the life of my friend." Lasar said, lowering the knife. "However, the Roman must die for what he has done. Secret or not, there must be blood."

"You will not kill my husband and take me back there." Tanaquil said furiously. She stepped away from the men and, thankfully, towards the edge of the roof and Julius. "I would rather die than be without him."

"See? He has tainted her already. She has to die with him." Lasar said. "We can tell her father that we had no choice. She cannot serve the temple in this state."

"I have no wish to serve in the temple. Not anymore." Tanaquil said, looking back at Julius with a smile that made his heart ache with its loveliness. "There are better things than the temple and I want explore them all."

"If she cannot serve your gods then why not let her live a life of joy?" Julius said, trying to reason with Quellus. He seemed to have greater conflict between his duty and his affection than the rest of the tribesmen. "Let her live Quellus."

He watched the man consider his words, consider what it would mean. When Quellus looked at Tanaquil his look softened and Julius was certain that they had won the day. The would be free and clear withing moments.

"She will live, Centurion, but it will not be with you." He picked up his bow and quickly pointed it at Julius again.

"What?" Julius said, looking at Tanaquil in confusion.

"Tanaquil, if you wish for him to live you will come back to the temple and live the life that you swore to, that you were chosen for." Quellus said, taking aim. "If you choose against this then you are free to live as his widow."

"Quellus, you cannot mean that." Tanaquil said.

There was so much despair in her voice that Julius ached to hold her. The cruelty of the man was nearly unbelievable. To make her choose between his life and her freedom was truly barbaric. If he were within reach Julius would have put his hands around Quellus neck and choked the life out him. The feelings that he had mistaken for affection were nothing more than pity for the agony that he was about to put her through.

"You must choose. Your freedom or his life?" Quellus said, locking his eyes with Julius.

He was certain that the other man meant to kill him and then take his broken-hearted wife back to the village regardless of his promise. Quellus wanted Julius dead, there was no doubt in the world about that. The feeling was mutual. Julius hated him for the lie and for putting Tanaquil through the agony of choosing. For forcing her to condemn him to death with the last words that he would hear from her lips in this life.

Julius could not allow her to suffer in that way. Not when there was a third option that no one else had yet considered, because it would be Julius making the sacrifice and not Tanaquil. They thought him to be a man of Rome and of greed. They would never consider that he might choose to make a sacrifice in order to spare her the pain of the choice.

"Quellus, please do not force this upon me. I beg you." Tanaquil cried, tears in her eyes.

"You must choose and choose now." He said with a shake of his head that brought tears to her eyes and a deeper rage to Julius' heart.

"No. I will make the choice." Julius said, loudly so that there could be no mistake, no taking it back. "I will choose so that she does not have to, you heartless bastard."

"Julius?" Tanaquil turned to face him, ignoring the bowmen to focus on him and their connection. "What do mean? What choice are you making?"

"I will go." Julius said, his voice shaking slightly. "I will go, you will stay and go with Quellus to the temple. In a short time, I will be finished my service to the legion. I will simply be a man of Rome. I will no longer be a soldier. I will come for you then and we will have our life together. I swear to you."

"You speak of leaving her behind and think that she would wait for you?" Quellus laughed. "Why would she do what you ask, Roman?"

"Love." Tanaquil said. "I will do it because I love him."

Julius could not help the soft smile that spread across his face when he heard her say the words out loud. He knew that she loved him, as he loved her. A declaration in public made that knowledge stronger. The wish to kiss her was so strong it hurt not to be able to touch her.

"I will go for the same reason that I will return. I leave my heart with you and when my service is complete I will return to the only one I trust with its safekeeping." Julius said, making sure that his words were directed to Tanaquil and her alone. The other men no longer mattered now that he knew that they would not harm her if she would leave with them.

"You are fools, both of you." Quellus said, lowering his bow and gesturing for the other to do the same. "I accept your terms. Tanaquil will stay and fulfill her duty. If the gods choose to punish her then that is their will, but it will not be done by any mortal man. You, Roman, will depart. If you return as a soldier then both your lives will be forfeit. Should you stay true to your word and return, no longer a soldier and without the power of the legion, then you may plead your cause to her father and our priests."

"No father that loves his daughter would deny the request of a man that loves her enough to leave everything and everyone he ever knew for the chance to be with his daughter." Julius said with a confidence he did not feel but had to pretend that he did. When the time came he would do and say whatever was needed to prove his worth and his love to the old man.

"Julius, please know that I will wait for you and you alone. There is no man that can steal my heart from you." Tanaquil said to him with tears in her eyes.

Her voice was brave and clear, but Julius saw the slight tremble in her hands and the quiver of her lip. She was just as unsure as he was and yet she had to know that this was the only chance that they both had at survival and a possible future together. It was agony and it was unbelievably cruel to them both, but it was the only solution that he could see. If he lied and tried to take Tanaquil again he had no doubt that one of the men would be tasked with ending her life before she could escape with him. Any further attempt to argue his right as husband would result in his own death by arrow, possibly hers as well if she tried to defend him.

This was the only way.

"I think it is time that you leave, Roman, before I change my mind." Quellus said, looking from one lover to the other. "Say your farewell and be gone."

A slight nod of his head was all the acknowledgment that Julius gave the other man, his eyes were fixed solely on his wife. The tears that were shining in her green eyes, made them more beautiful than any emerald that Julius had ever seen. She reached a hand towards him, as though the distance between them was only so wide as the span of their arms and began to speak in a voice that grew shakier with each word she spoke.

"Julius, I never knew that I could want to be anything more than a priestess. Never did I consider a future as a wife or dream of becoming a mother. That changed when I met you and now is all I desire in this life. Your courage and calm despite captivity inspired me. The strength of your heart, how you did not let yourself become bitter or broken, touched my heart. There is no future that I desire without you in it, beside me. I will wait for you until we meet again, in this life or the next."

She looked as though she would crumble. Each of the tears on her face were like a stab to his heart, but this was the only way, the honorable way, to do what was needed so that they could be together.

"Tanaquil, you need to know that if not for the interference of these men there is nothing that would have stopped us from sharing all the days of our lives together. There are so many promises that I made to you that must now be delayed. I swear to you that when I return I will spend the rest of my life making up to you for the time that we have lost. We will have our life together. All of those things that I told you that we would do, as soon as I can get released from my obligation to the legion, we will begin that beautiful adventure together. I will come back to find you. I love you and I will love you for all the rest of my life." Julius could hear the tremor in his own voice as he continued. "There is no joy in my life, no true joy, without your laugh in my ears. There is no tenderness I crave that is not the soft brush of your lips against mine. There is nothing and no one who can touch my heart as you have. I will love no one but you in this life."

In that moment he thought that the gods might give him wings to leap across the divide to hold Tanaquil. The pull of her eyes was that strong. Julius took a small step towards the edge of the roof, trying to be as close to her as he could in those final moments. His heart was beating so fast and loud in his chest that he was surprised that the others did not hear it. The voice of Quellus cut through the agonizing silence and broke the magic of the moment.

"Enough flowery words. You have said your farewell. Now, be gone from sight and from this city before I see fit to change my mind and let loose my arrow."

The temporary victory seemed to have given a thrill of false power to the other man, but Julius knew that this was not the time for that confrontation to take place. When he returned to recover his wife there would be a reckoning between the two men that would be unforgettable.

"When we meet again, Quellus, do not think that you will find me so compliant. We will stand equals that day and the debt between us will be balanced." Julius said, shaking his head and shouldering the bag of few belongings that would now be cherished for the memories they held of his wife.

"Tanaquil, I will return for you, my love. Hold to that truth and do not despair."

When she nodded her and blew a kiss towards him Julius turned but her voice stopped him.

"Julius? Take this with you." Tanaquil said, pulling the pendant from around her neck and tossing it across the divide to him.

The smooth blue stone was warm from resting on her skin. He draped it around his neck, bowed his head towards her and departed the roof. The owners seemed to be shocked by his presence, but they did not move against him. Whether it was his grief, or the townspeople knew that what had nearly happened in their village Julius was never sure. He did not see another soul as he made his way out, towards home. It was hours of walking later that the reality of his choice, his loss, and the weight of his heartbreak, finally brought Julius to his knees.

When the dawn came he rose from the ground with the sun in his eyes and a fire of determination burning in his heart. No matter what it took, when his service to the legion was complete, he would come back for his wife. Their lives would be all the richer for the delay and their love would be as boundless as their freedom.

Epilogue:

It had been more than five years since Julius had scouted the crest of this hill with the other men in his unit. It had been that long since he had been taken as a captive, since he had looked into the eyes that would change his life forever. Now, as dawn approached, he would walk down the hill with pride. The people at his side, friends that were not soldiers of the Republic, had traveled with him all the way from Rome to make sure that this reunion happened.

He knew that if anything went wrong, if he were greeted with violence, betrayal or if his heart were broken he would not suffer it alone. He had warriors beside him, men that commanded respect by their presence alone. Quellus and his type would be fools to risk an altercation now. Julius and his would subdue or end them as was needed.

"Come." The man at his side said, with a smile. "Let us see the woman you spoke of. I would see if your words were enough to describe her beauty or if this is yet another thing in which I stand your superior."

"There would have to a first thing you were superior in for this to be added to any list you keep trapped in that fevered mind of yours." Julius laughed, clapping him on the shoulder. "Come so that you might see that there are no words yet spoken capable of describing the beauty of my wife."

"So says every man." Another companion said, laughing loud enough to draw the attention of those at the bottom of the hill.

"Only the wise ones, my friend." A softer voice said, with a tender touch to his arm before whispering in his ear. "Go to her. She is waiting."

Julius looked down the hill to find that there was indeed a woman staring at the group at the top of the hill. She had wildly flying red hair and was slowly walking towards the bottom of the hill. Moving to meet her, his heart was racing beneath the simple tunic he wore. He knew that the others would follow him down the hill, giving him enough space to have a moment of privacy with the woman who had held his heart exclusively for years.

"Tanaquil?" He said, pausing a few steps away from her. "I know that I have been gone longer than either of us could have foreseen, it could not be helped. If you give me the chance I will do my best to explain it."

"I do not need your explanation, Julius. I thought that you would be gone for merely months, not years. So many things have changed." She said.

Her eyes were flashing, and he thought that she would tell him to leave. Then her face softened as did her voice when she closed the distance between them to throw her arms around him.

"My love for you is not among them though."

He held her close, lowering his mouth to hers to claim a kiss so powerful it turned day to night and left him seeing stars at its end.

"Tanaquil, my beloved wife, I would like for you to meet my companions, my family, the men that stand as my brothers." Julius said, gesturing to those gathered behind him.

"It would be a great honor, husband, to meet them." She said with a smile that grew until it had spread across her entire face. "First I must introduce you to the one who has been my constant companion since shortly after you left."

Julius prepared himself to meet a priest or priestess, one of the women of the village or even another man. When a child with dark hair and green eyes stepped forward instead he was confused. Turning his head to Tanaquil he began to ask who he was supposed to meet when he saw her put her hand upon the child's head.

"Julius Lucius, meet your son, Jamus. Greet your father, my son, he has returned to us at last."

He dropped to his knees before the child, his child, trying to find words to greet the boy he could never have imagined existed.

"Greetings father." The little boy said, his voice small but strong. "I have done my best while we waited for your return. I hope you will be proud of me."

It was obvious in the way that the boy and his mother looked at him that they had been tormented in Julius' absence. It was a wrong that he would see put right before the day was through.

"Oh, my son." He opened his arms to welcome the child with an embrace. "You are my pride and joy. I am sure that you have been a good man of the house, but I will take that responsibility now."

He stood with his son on his arm and reached for the hand of his wife.

"Things will be different now. Your father is home to stay."

www.ingramcontent.com/pod-product-compliance
Lightning Source LLC
Chambersburg PA
CBHW030541180626
46810CB00005B/1964